Ibaza

WHEN HARRIET MET SOJOURNER

By CATHERINE CLINTON • Illustrated by SHANE W. EVANS

KATHERINE TEGEN BOOKS

An Imprint of HarperCollinsPublishers

Amistad

Dedicated to Julie & Carla Anne and Deborah & Jody,

because we make new friends but keep the old—and you are my silver and my gold.

—C.C.

Thank you, God. Dedicated to my daughter, Yurie.

—S.W.E.

Photo of Sojourner Truth courtesy of the Library of Congress, LC-USZ62-119343
Photo of Harriet Tubman courtesy of the Library of Congress, LC-USZ62-7816

Amistad is an imprint of HarperCollins Publishers.

Library of Congress Cataloging-in-Publication Data
Clinton, Catherine, 1952–
    When Harriet met Sojourner / by Catherine Clinton ; illustrated by Shane W. Evans. — 1st ed.
        p.   cm.
    ISBN-10: 0-06-050425-0 (trade bdg.) — ISBN-13: 978-0-06-050425-0 (trade bdg.)
    ISBN-10: 0-06-050426-9 (lib. bdg.) — ISBN-13: 978-0-06-050426-7 (lib. bdg.)
    1. Tubman, Harriet, 1820?–1913—Juvenile literature. 2. Truth, Sojourner, d. 1883—Juvenile literature. 3. African Americans—Biography—
Juvenile literature. 4. African American women—Biography—Juvenile literature. 5. Slaves—United States—Biography—Juvenile literature. 6. African
American abolitionists—Biography—Juvenile literature. 7. Social reformers—United States—Biography—Juvenile literature. 8. Boston (Mass.)—
History—Civil War, 1861–1865—Juvenile literature. I. Evans, Shane, ill. II. Title.
E444.T82C58 2007   2006019099
973.7'1150922—dc22
[B]

Typography by Sarah Hoy
1 2 3 4 5 6 7 8 9 10
❖
First Edition

When America was young, young and new and wanting to be free . . . not everyone in America was free. Although it was a land of promise—yes, a land of real promise—not all promises were kept.

Two strong, brave black women wanted America to fulfill its promises to allow each and every American to be born free and live in a land of equal opportunity.

This is their story, the story of Harriet Tubman and Sojourner Truth and how their paths crossed. . . .

Sojourner Truth was born first—some day, sometime around 1797, near the Hudson Valley, in upstate New York. She was born the daughter of enslaved parents, parents owned by a wealthy Dutch planter. They gave her the name Isabella, and she took her father's name, Bomefree.

Isabella Bomefree—Bomefree, but not free.

Bomefree means "tall tree" in Dutch. The name suited Isabella well. She grew strong and tall, bending like a willow while working the fields alongside her twelve brothers and sisters.

As the crow flies hundreds of miles south from Isabella's birthplace, it might alight on the eastern shore of Maryland, where sometime around 1825 a young slave girl named Araminta was born.

Araminta's parents loved and cherished their sons and daughters but could not protect them from the evils of slavery.

Two of her sisters were snatched away, stolen off and sold South—they were gone but never forgotten.

Araminta dreamed of freedom, of flying away with her whole family. She did not know how or when but yearned for flight. One day, in freedom, she would be known as Harriet Tubman.

Isabella this and Isabella that! Forced to obey a parade of masters, from dawn to dusk. Sent from farm to farm, away from her brothers and sisters, away from her parents. Poor Isabella.

Once she was sent to a farm where they spoke only English. She spoke Dutch and could not understand, could not make herself understood.

She tried and tried to be good and obedient, and everyone knew she was a good worker. But an English master called her names—and even beat her.

She vowed when she grew up, she would leave slavery behind and be poor Isabella no more. She would defeat those who had tried to defeat her, and rename herself Sojourner Truth.

Araminta, too, worked hard, moving from one master to another, hired out from the age of seven. But one day when one of her friends from the fields was trying to get away from an angry overseer, Araminta tried to protect him. When the overseer threw a heavy piece of lead, it hit Araminta instead of her friend—smashing in her skull and knocking her to the ground. She was almost killed!

Carried home half-dead, Araminta was nursed by her mother, who sat by her daughter's bedside and told Bible stories—of David and Goliath, of Daniel in the lion's den, of Moses and the Red Sea. It was nearly a miracle when she finally recovered. But Harriet's scar would always be with her, a reminder of slavery's evils and a symbol of her courage and willingness to help others.

Isabella grew and grew until she was six feet tall. She was one of the strongest workers in the field, and not a man could best her! She worked hard, but a yearning for freedom rose like sap within her. She married another slave and had five children, her daughters and son like branches reaching from her sturdy trunk.

When New York passed a law outlawing slavery after 1827, Isabella thought that God had answered her prayers. Her master promised to free her in a year. She counted the months and weeks and days until she might leave slavery behind.

Araminta hungered for freedom as well. She lived in fear of the auction block. One of her loved ones or she herself might be put up for sale, sold to the highest bidder and shipped off, never to be seen again.

So like the quilt she worked on, one square at a time, she pieced together her plans for running off to the North. It took patience and skill. It took listening and learning. She needed reliable advice about an escape route. She had great faith, faith she was made for bigger things. And she knew she would find those things, once she crossed over from slavery to freedom.

Isabella patiently waited twelve long months before asking her master to emancipate her. When she finally confronted him, her owner broke his promise and said she must stay enslaved, just a little longer.

But Isabella was tired of waiting, and broke the chains herself. She walked out and left slavery behind.

When her master illegally sold her son away, she went to court to win him back. Isabella became a tower of strength for family and friends. When she gave herself a new name, Sojourner Truth, it symbolized that she felt born again, born into freedom and committed to helping others find freedom.

When Araminta's master died in 1849, all she could think was: sold away, sold away—she was going to be sold away, just like her sisters. So within months of her owner's death, Araminta stole off from her Maryland home. It was hard to leave her family behind, hard to leave her husband, John Tubman, but she feared it was now or never! The midnight sky and silent stars were her only companions on her flight to freedom.

After she made it safely north, she found a community to welcome her and took a new name, a freedom name. She took the name Harriet, which was her mother's name. As Harriet Tubman, she was finally free—and as Harriet Tubman, she would become a legendary leader for those seeking freedom.

Sojourner Truth preached and lectured all over the North, from the shores of Massachusetts to Ohio's fruited plains. She made stirring appeals to emancipate both slaves and women, and her deep, booming voice cast a spell over listeners.

Once, when a man told the audience that women were weak and needed protection, that women couldn't take care of themselves, Sojourner Truth got angry. She stood up, all six feet of her, and held out her arm, an arm made strong by years of slave labor, and asked: "Aren't I a woman?"

Harriet Tubman was only five feet tall but became a giant among her people by working with the Underground Railroad, the network of blacks and whites who secretly guided runaways to safety. It was not a railroad, nor was it underground— but it was a powerful resistance movement, trying to defeat unjust laws.

Harriet dodged bloodhounds and bounty hunters, guiding many escaped slaves all the way to Canada. She told her admirers, "I never lost a passenger!" Harriet became the most famous Underground Railroad conductor in the years leading up to the Civil War.

When the Civil War began in 1861, both Sojourner Truth and Harriet Tubman continued their campaigns against slavery.

Tall, fiery Sojourner gave speeches across the North, heating up her audiences to convince men to enlist in the federal army, to join the battle to defeat the Confederates. She was a staunch defender of the Union cause.

Harriet Tubman, cool and collected, worked as a spy behind enemy lines in South Carolina. With an iron nerve, projecting a sense of calm before the storm, she led men in uniform on midnight raids, ignoring the danger, as she always had.

When Sojourner Truth was on a speaking tour in the fall of 1864, she stopped off in Boston for a visit. It just so happened that Harriet Tubman was in Boston as well, taking time off from her wartime duties in the occupied South.

No one took notes or reported on the meeting at the time, so we can only imagine what they might have said to one another. . . .

After hearing about one another for so many years, they must have warmly embraced, as if finding a long-lost relative. The tall one wore glasses and spoke with a Dutch accent, while the short one still had some of her southern drawl. But they were connected by a kinship that went deeper than language, perhaps even deeper than blood—a kinship of spirit.

They had much to offer one another, because Sojourner had been fighting slavery for a lot longer than Harriet. Yet even though she was decades younger, Harriet had many adventures to share— carrying slaves to freedom on the Underground Railroad and fighting Confederates, exploits Sojourner would have wanted to hear about.

When their paths crossed in Boston that October day in 1864, there was no photographer to record the occasion, no newspaper interview to highlight this historic meeting. And when they parted, Harriet and Sojourner did not know if they would ever see one another again. But sharing stories built a friendship, with the memory of time together keeping them close—even when miles apart.

It was a memory these legendary women carried with them for the rest of their days. Sister Harriet! Sister Sojourner! Together at last!

EPILOGUE

Sojourner Truth met with President Lincoln at the White House on October 29, 1864, the first black woman leader to be so honored. She remained in Washington to work for the Freedman's Hospital and other charitable causes. When Truth returned to her home and family in Battle Creek, Michigan, after the war, she continued her work for women's rights and racial reform. She died on November 26, 1883, and her funeral was one of the biggest Battle Creek had ever seen.

Harriet Tubman returned to her household in Auburn, New York, after the war ended, and dedicated her life to helping others. She opened up a charity home for veterans and orphans, for the disabled and homeless. Her Harriet Tubman Home was dedicated only a few years before her death on March 10, 1913, in Auburn. She was buried with military honors. A bronze plaque honoring her life and legacy, dedicated in 1914, remains on the local county courthouse.

For Beth Ann, Sean, and Eric,
grand niece and nephews, indeed! –K.N.

For Thomas and Edie –L.W.

STERLING CHILDREN'S BOOKS
New York

An Imprint of Sterling Publishing
387 Park Avenue South
New York, NY 10016

STERLING CHILDREN'S BOOKS and the distinctive Sterling Children's Books logo
are trademarks of Sterling Publishing Co., Inc.

Text © 2013 by Kim Norman
Illustrations © 2013 by Liza Woodruff

Designed by Elizabeth Phillips

The illustrations were created using watercolor, colored pencil, and pastel.

ISBN 978-1-4549-0384-0

Library of Congress Cataloging-in-Publication Data

Norman, Kimberly.
  If it's snowy and you know it, clap your paws / by Kim Norman ; illustrated by
Liza Woodruff.
    p. cm.
  Summary: Animals enjoy a variety of wintry activities in the snow.
  ISBN 978-1-4549-0384-0 (hardcover)
  [1. Stories in rhyme. 2. Animals--Fiction. 3. Snow--Fiction. 4. Winter--Fiction.]
  I. Woodruff, Liza, ill. II. Title. III. Title: If it is snowy and you know it.
  PZ8.3.N7498If 2013
  [E]--dc23

              2012014460

Distributed in Canada by Sterling Publishing
c/o Canadian Manda Group, 165 Dufferin Street
Toronto, Ontario, Canada M6K 3H6
Distributed in the United Kingdom by GMC Distribution Services
Castle Place, 166 High Street, Lewes, East Sussex, England BN7 1XU
Distributed in Australia by Capricorn Link (Australia) Pty. Ltd.
P.O. Box 704, Windsor, NSW 2756, Australia

For information about custom editions, special sales, and premium and corporate purchases,
please contact Sterling Special Sales at 800-805-5489 or specialsales@sterlingpublishing.com.

Manufactured in China
Lot #:
2 4 6 8 10 9 7 5 3 1
04/13

www.sterlingpublishing.com/kids

If It's Snowy and You Know It, Clap Your Paws!

by
Kim Norman

illustrated by
Liza Woodruff

STERLING CHILDREN'S BOOKS
New York

If it's snowy and you know it, clap your paws.
You can tumble on the tundra, just because.
If it's snowy and you know it,
roll a snowball up and throw it.
If it's snowy and you know it . . .

. . . clap your paws!

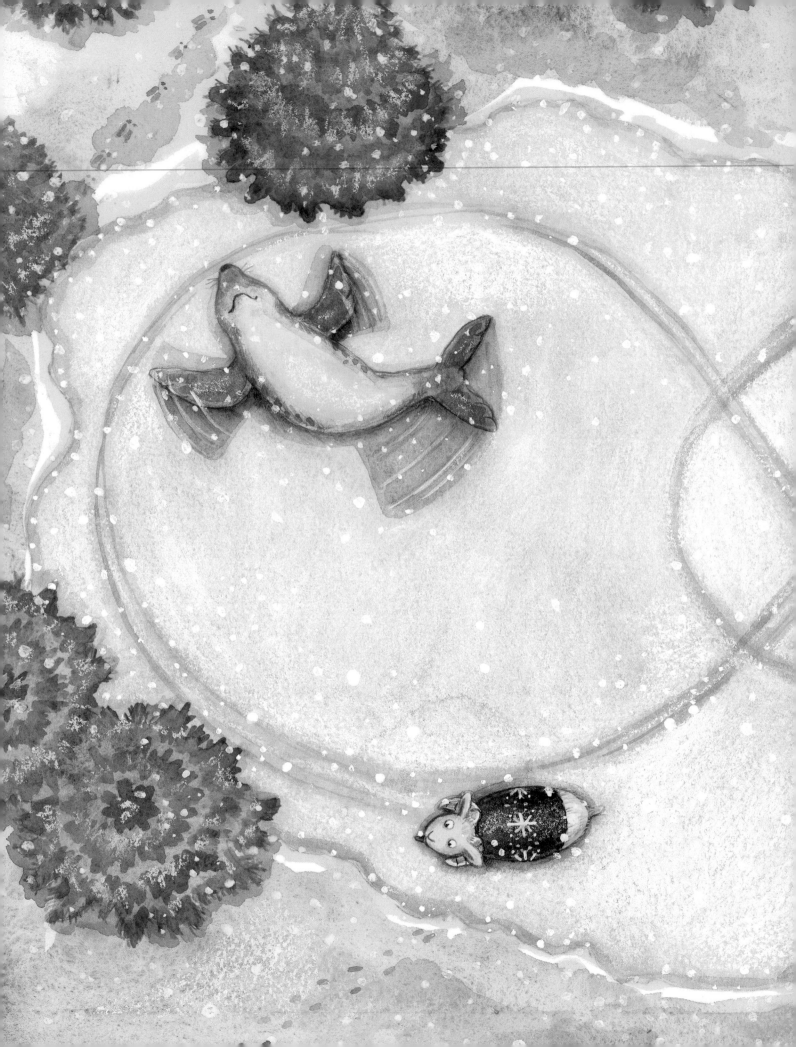

If your fur is full of flurries, taste a flake.
Skate around or make some angels on a lake.
If your fur is full of flurries,
you'll forget your winter worries.
If your fur is full of flurries...

...taste a flake!

CRASH

If the skies are crisp and clearing, grab your skis.
Give your tiny friends a ride behind your knees.
If the skies are crisp and clearing,
let a walrus do the steering.
If the skies are crisp and clearing...

...grab your skis!

If it's shimmery and sunny, sculpt a friend.
If he topples, it's an easy job to mend.
If it's shimmery and sunny,
borrow glasses from the bunny.
If it's shimmery and sunny...

...sculpt a friend!

If it's frosty and you're freezing, build a fort,
leaving room for all your buddies, tall or short.
If it's frosty and you're freezing,
add some curtains that are pleasing.
If it's frosty and you're freezing...

...build a fort!

If it's drafty and you're drifting, give a roar.
Get some help from white belugas off the shore.
If it's drafty and you're drifting,
hail a whale for heavy lifting.
If it's drafty and you're drifting…

If at last you're finally landing, blow a kiss.

Make a promise that you'll write to friends you'll miss.

If at last you're finally landing,

leave the float you've been commanding.

If at last you're finally landing...

If it's starry and you're starving, share a meal.
There's enough for all, from caribou to seal.
If it's starry and you're starving,
add a sparkly iceberg carving.
If it's starry and you're starving...

...share a meal!

If it's arctic and you're aching, soak your toes.
Hold a steamy cup of cocoa to your nose.
If it's arctic and you're aching,
give your paws a gentle baking.
If it's arctic and you're aching...

...soak your toes.

If it's wintry and you're weary, go inside.
Paint a picture of the icy sports you tried.
If it's wintry and you're weary,
read a book that's warm and cheery.
If it's wintry and you're weary...

...go inside.

If it's sleeting and you're sleepy, climb in bed.
Tuck your tails and paws and fins beneath the spread.
If it's sleeting and you're sleepy,
snuggle up with something sheepy.
There's a world of wild adventures...

...in your head!

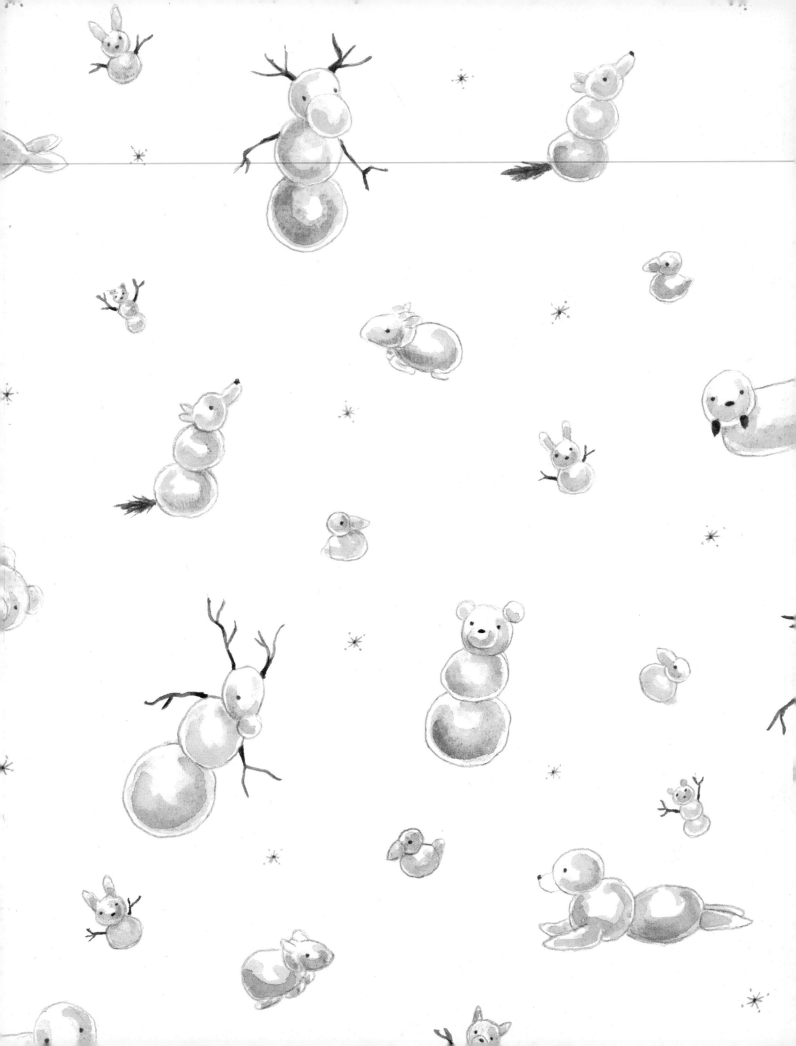